The Reunion

by Dan Stalp
and
Jim Mathis

The Reunion

Jim Mathis

11035 W 96th Pl

Overland Park, KS 66214

Jim@MathisPhoto.net

Second printing

Printed in the United States of America

www.TheReunionBook.us

ISBN: 978-0-9773055-4-4

TABLE OF
CONTENTS

Introduction

Many people take a look at their lives as their high school class reunions approach – particularly if 20 or more years have passed. Some classmates are eager to attend because they are proud of who they are and look forward to rekindling friendships. More classmates struggle with whether to attend because it's a reminder of who they were or who they have not become.

The four main characters of "The Reunion" are Gary Davidson, Ben Michaels, Kevin Brown, and Elizabeth Fitzpatrick. They all graduated from high school together in West Plaines, Kansas. West Plaines is a small town where everybody knows everybody – even their dog's names. That doesn't mean that everybody is best friends or even that everybody likes everybody, but you tend to get along or leave.

Gary Davidson is single, eccentric, tall and lean, with long hair and a scruffy beard. After graduating from high school, Gary went on to the University of Kansas on an art scholarship. He got a Master's of Fine Arts degree and stayed in Lawrence, mainly hanging out, doing odd jobs to support himself, and of course, painting.

Ben Michaels is divorced, outgoing, and has jet black hair and funky glasses. After graduating from high school, Ben went on to the University of Chicago. He had a fun time in college and eventually received a degree in business. He loves Chicago, but is struggling with raising two small children after a recent divorce.

Kevin Brown is married, a former athlete, who always has a ball cap on. After graduating from high school, Kevin stayed in West Plaines working construction until he started his own construction company. He is happily married with a growing family, living life very simply.

Elizabeth Fitzpatrick is married, attractive, and bold, the cheerleader type in high school. After graduating from high school, she received a scholarship to the University of Colorado in business. Her degree was not wasted and she has done very well, living the life of a successful executive in suburban Denver. She has a stressful marriage due to some choices she and her husband continue to make.

Read along as we check in with each classmate as they are heading back to West Plaines to attend their twentieth high school reunion.

Chapter 1 – Going Home

Gary Davidson

Wow, has it really been twenty years since I've seen the old gang? I wonder what has happened to Elizabeth. The last I heard she was working on her MBA. And I guess Kevin still lives in my hometown of West Plaines, Kansas. His mother mentioned that she saw him every now and then at school events. But I am most concerned about myself. What have I done with my life these past twenty years since high school?

As I drove through the Flint Hills and across the prairie to the reunion, a thousand images passed through my head. Images from the past, hanging out at the corner store, sneaking cigarettes, or trying to get somebody to buy some "hard stuff" from the liquor store. I remember the art class from high school where I was such a star. Mrs. Whetstone was very encouraging and was almost certainly instrumental in me getting that scholarship to KU. If it hadn't been for her, I'd probably be painting cars in West Plaines. Actually I'd be a lot better off if I was painting cars. Those guys make good money. Why didn't I stay like my dad wanted me to?

Back in West Plaines, I was the weird kid who liked to draw and had all the decals and bumper stickers on my car. I was also the only kid in my high school who drove a Checker. I bought it from a Wichita cab company for $250, but it ran great and even got me back and forth to Lawrence a few times. Too bad Checker went out of business. They could have sold a ton of them if they hadn't been so focused on taxi companies. There was never any attempt to make them attractive, only durable. Some redesigned bodywork and a few nods to fashion probably would have saved the company from bankruptcy, since their reputation for dependability and long life was well known.

Anyway, in Lawrence I found out that I wasn't so weird after all. Everybody loved that old Checker with the huge back seat, and my first art show got some good reviews, if no sales.

I had some success throwing pots. They had sold well at a few art fairs, at least well enough to buy a kiln and more clay. Everybody loved my work, but there were only a few takers. I love the feel of the clay in my hands, the smells and the textures, but it seemed like a lot work, just to sit under a hot tent and sell a few $20 items when the rent is $650 a month.

Painting definitely is more appealing. Just last year I had a $2,000 commission, and there could be another one this year. That gallery in Santa Fe seemed pretty certain they could sell a few paintings, but I would have to deliver them or ship them to be sold on consignment. Maybe I'll just drive on down to Santa Fe after the reunion and get a feel for the place. I could certainly use some inspiration, and I am pretty sure the old Subaru is up to it, if I can get some gas money somewhere.

I remember my classmates from high school. There were people who couldn't draw a straight line with good paying jobs in the city. People like Ben Michaels; what a joke. They have new houses, new cars, and beautiful families. Hah, they wouldn't know a good painting if they saw one. I know people who made a hundred grand a year who bought $50 paintings because they matched their carpet. The idea makes me both sad and mad at the same time.

What is wrong with this country when talented people like me are starving and the Philistines are getting rich?

It will be interesting to see how many of the old gang are still in town and which ones followed their dreams and got out. How many of them, like me, have followed their dreams down a dead end street? And how did I get on this dead end street in the first place? Was it because I wouldn't play the system? People tell me I need to put on a suit and talk to people who could afford my stuff, but that just isn't my style. Maybe it was the grass. But I have never even been busted. Surely it isn't affecting me in any negative way. It was just the "system." The whole stinking system conspires to keep the truly creative and talented people in their place. It has always been that way.

The people who are considered the great masters were not received well in their day and many died paupers. That will probably be my fate as well. Yes, I would have the last say from the grave. Years from now, people will be reading about me and saying what a pity it was that I was not understood in my own time. My only duty now is to make art that will stand the test of time. But how will I know, and do I even care?

West Plaines - 50 miles. Oh yes, the reunion. Why am I even going? Those people didn't like me in high school and certainly will not like me now. With my long hair, straggly beard, and thrift store clothes, I am hardly the picture of success. Why am I giving my old classmates the pleasure of saying, "We knew he wouldn't amount to anything."

Maybe I should have my MFA degree tattooed on my chest so people will know I did something. But the day I received my Master's of Fine Arts, the lead story in the local paper was a lost dog. Big deal. Nobody in that town cares about things like this.

Back in Lawrence my friends are mostly in the same boat: talented artists, musicians, actors, and writers. The lucky ones are waiting tables or making lattes and paying the rent. The unlucky ones are crashing with friends or living on the streets. Most still are waiting for the "break," the big sale, the hit song, best seller, or the $100,000 commission that never comes.

Twenty-five miles; time to put on a happy face and tell everybody how great it is to be a big time artist, following your dreams and changing the world.

Ben Michaels

I am really looking forward to attending this reunion! If it's anything like our 10-year reunion, bring it on! I had them rolling at the reunion with all my jokes. I am sure I've still got it!

I qualified for an upgrade to an SUV at the Kansas City airport to drive to West Plaines. They don't even sell cars like this in West Plaines. I am actually a little self conscious about it. Ten years ago, I wouldn't have been.

Chicago has been great for me. I have had so much fun there. I love working downtown on LaSalle Street in the financial district at an up and coming financial advisory firm. It's a long commute from Evanston, but that's life in the fast lane. The financial business provides me good money, golf a couple times a week, and a country club membership. Life is good!

I was single when I went to my 10-year class reunion and brought my now ex-wife with me. Weird to think our marriage just ended last summer after nine years. I'm not really crazy about explaining that to everyone.

I guess that is one of the consequences to the life I have led. This divorce has brought me to my knees. While I know I have changed, I'm really struggling with the old me versus the new me.

Speaking of the new me, I'm really glad Laura is coming with me. I feel good with Laura on my arm. I have lost 35 pounds since the divorce and Laura looks great. I'd like to think our relationship is more than how we look. I feel more different on the inside than the outside these days.

You know who I would like to see again? Gary Davidson. In high school I didn't even know who this "cat" was. I mean I knew who he was, but I'm not sure I even talked to the guy once! At our 10-year reunion, we struck up a conversation and I remember liking his "energy." He didn't have all the "stuff" I had, but he seemed at peace with himself. He was doing what he loved and he didn't seem to have as much stress as I did.

Man, I really have a lot of stress now with a big mortgage, alimony, and now my relationship with Laura. Feels like a "hamster wheel" to me.

Oh, I have to remember to tell everyone about the radio show I've been doing in Chicago! When I do the radio show, I feel like I'm in my element and I'm good at it!

I remember in 1st grade when we had our first class play for the school talent show. Our play was "Little House on the Prairie," and I played the lead role as Pa Ingalls. I was nervous at first, yet so many parents and older kids in the school told me what a great job I did. I was hooked after that – and that is how I feel on my radio show.

Too bad it's a small station with only 10,000 listeners, but a man's got to start somewhere. On the other hand, that is more than the population in West Plaines.

There is nothing like downtown Chicago with the electricity and energy. I would love to meet Oprah, because I could totally see myself doing what she does.

If I did become a talk show host, what would happen to all my clients in the financial advisory business? I do like helping my clients and I have fun doing it. How many people can say they really enjoy their financial advisor meetings? I know that answer – none! Except my clients - they tell me that all the time!

I'm trying to remember who still lives in West Plaines. Mom talks about a couple of families. I think she said Kevin Brown is still there. Now there was a wild man! He must be doing pretty well because I think he and his company built that new little subdivision north of town. I think he even lives there – the Beverly Hills of West Plaines!

You know who I heard was "knocking it out of the park" was Elizabeth. She was voted most likely to succeed and from all I've heard - she is. I was voted least likely to succeed our senior year – what's up with that?

While I'm nervous about this weekend, it is going to be a riot! West Plaines, here we come!

Kevin Brown

I looked at my calendar. The red circle around August 25th tells me that the high school reunion is this weekend. All *those* people will be back. In some ways I look forward to the reunion because it reminds me of all the fun we had in high school. I remember the good times hanging out after school, dragging Main, and playing football.

I was a good football player and that catch in the last minute to win the game that sent us to the state championship is still mentioned every now and then down at Casey's. Of course, eight-man football doesn't get much attention from the big colleges. I had no offers and there was certainly no other way I would have been able to go on to college.

Anyway, I am just glad to have made it through high school, get a job, and be on my own. I know of classmates who went on to college and came back to live with their parents. What a bunch of losers. I am glad I learned how to work. There is a lot to be said for not being afraid to get your hands dirty.

Sue Ellen, who was a year behind me in school, moved in with me after she left home and we were married before the first baby was born. Sue Ellen has been a cashier at Walmart ever since and seems to like it, but she doesn't say much about it. The kids and school activities keep her busy when she isn't working.

It would be nice if I could get a better paying job so she could stay home with the kids, but that isn't going to happen. There are half a dozen Hispanics waiting for my job as it is. Besides, $15 an hour is pretty much top wage in West Plaines and I am lucky to be working at all.

Every now and then people will ask me about my plans and what I am going to do in the future. When I think of the future, I can't get past next weekend when I will be able to get on my bike and ride. My big, long-term dreams? That's easy… a new motorcycle.

Those young guys with the crotch rockets look pretty cool, but that isn't my style. I couldn't bring myself to even think about a rice-burner. All the people I know are Harley guys. Harley-Davidson is the ultimate ride. So what if some people think they are heavy and clumsy? When you are born to ride, there isn't anything else. Even this old Harley is still a Harley.

I missed Sturgis again this year. Maybe next year I won't have to work and will be able to ride north with the guys. The time I went five years ago was a blast and I have been wanting to go back ever since.

Sue Ellen isn't into bikes all that much, but she doesn't mind me doing whatever I want to do on weekends. After all, I work hard all week and need to cut loose every now and then.

Maybe I will be able to reconnect with some of the people I knew in school at the reunion. Ben Michaels went off to Chicago and nobody has heard from him since. That is surprising because he was such a show-off in high school, always wanting the newest and the best of everything. He was always talking about how great he was going to be, how he would be famous some day.

Did he really have the only BMW in West Plaines, or was that someone else? Knowing Ben, it was probably somebody else's and he claimed it was his. Anyway, he probably thinks he is too good for West Plaines, but somebody said that they heard he was coming. He'll probably be driving an Escalade or something.

And crazy Gary Davidson, he was the nut that was always drawing pictures and making stuff that he claimed was sculpture. He went to KU on an art scholarship and, as far as we know, he is still there. That old Checker was a hoot. It will be interesting to see if anybody has seen him.

Then there were the "cool" kids like Elizabeth Fitzpatrick. She is usually here during the holidays when she visits her parents. She lives in Denver and appears to be doing well. She was one of the smart ones who got out of West Plaines. She will probably be here because she likes to come back and check on her parents. Her dad is not doing well, so she doesn't miss many opportunities to spend time with them.

At any rate, it will be interesting to see who shows up.

Elizabeth Fitzpatrick

I cannot believe I am nearly 40 years old and have been out of school 20 years. It seems like yesterday - we were "making Mains," drinking beer out at the two mile county road, and of course chasing the cute guys…

I wasn't that interested in many of the boys in my class. Having seven brothers and sisters in my family and being the fifth kid, I tended to like the upper classmen. The only guy in my class I was attracted to was Ben Michaels. Not so much on looks, but was he funny. I've always liked that in a guy – the ones who could make me laugh.

I'm looking forward to the class reunion because I have really done well for myself. I earned my CPA right out of school, got my dream job at an oil company in Denver, got married at age 24 to my college sweetheart and have two kids – a son and a daughter. Just perfect! Or is it?

Bill has been a great husband for the past 14 years and provider (not that he needs to make a lot of money with my income), but he does travel a lot. Because he is in sales for another oil company in Denver, he "has to" entertain a lot in addition to his travel. It always seems like alcohol is involved in the golf trips, fishing trips, etc. I'm a little concerned about his drinking to be really honest. Personally, I think my dad was an alcoholic and now wonder if history is repeating itself?

Speaking of Dad, I really need to check on him and Mom when I'm back in West Plaines. Mom is 69 and Dad is 77. Dad was recently diagnosed with prostate cancer and I'm not sure how aggressively they plan to treat him. Plus, they have been in the same house for over 22 years. A five-bedroom house may be too big for just the two of them.

I wonder if Kevin Brown will attend. He's the only guy I really dated in high school, if you can count four months dating. He really wasn't my personality type, but he was interested in me. I was a cheerleader and he was a jock – so it seemed like the thing to do.

You know what I would love to know, but there is no way to know? What everyone's W-2 earnings were for last year? Gosh, I sound like a materialistic you know what! Having said that, I bet I'm in the top one or two. Hey – I have earned every penny.

Good thing I'm organized, because my kids are getting to the age where it's getting busy. Melissa is 8 and we already have her in competitive soccer and dance. Bill already has Aaron playing hockey. Man is that an expensive sport! Oh well, that's why we work as hard as we do. I never had the opportunity to do all this stuff – not with eight kids in my family. I don't want them to go without like I did.

Well, I better go shopping at Cherry Hills today to get that perfect dress to wear. Reunions are only every 10 years, right?

Chapter 1 discussion questions:

What are your first impressions of Gary, Ben, Kevin, and Elizabeth?

_____

_____

Which one can you most closely identify with, or would you be friends with? Why?

_____

_____

Which one would you have the least in common with? Why?

_____

_____

Chapter 2 – West Plaines

Gary Davidson

Well, here I am in West Plaines. First stop, the old Town Tavern. I can't believe this place is still here. In fact, the funny thing about West Plaines is that nothing ever seems to change. Every time I stop here, it seems like I pick up right where I left off the last time I was here. It is some sort of a time warp or something.

I also forget how much of my work has been affected by growing up in a place like this. Artists who come from big cities, or even medium-sized towns, miss out on a lot of the little things that can only happen in a small town. I guess there is a little bit of Norman Rockwell in me, as much as I hate to admit it.

I don't think about it much until I see an old pick-up in a field or beside a barn and realize that there is a very similar image in one of my paintings. I didn't even realize where it came from. We are all so influenced by our roots in ways that we don't even know.

I walked into the tavern. Well, it is actually just an old bar. I don't know where the word "tavern" came from. I think the guy who started this place back in the fifties was trying to make it sound a little classier. Not that "tavern" is any classier sounding than "bar," but hey, he was trying. Anyway the first person I saw was Kevin Brown. Kevin is one of the regulars and has never left town. He is a nice guy and sort of epitomizes small-town life. He has a couple of kids, his wife is a cashier at Walmart, and Kevin works construction jobs when he can. Sue Ellen is as sweet as she can be. I guess she is content just standing behind a counter all day and raising a family.

Kevin seems very happy just hanging out and being with his friends. I think there is something to be said for that, but I always wanted to leave my mark on the world. I think it has something to do with trying to be immortal. We are all going to die, but I want to leave something behind when I go – something worthwhile.

I don't care about money or having a lot of stuff, but years from now I want people to point to something I created and say, "That guy was good."

The other one of my classmates at the Town Tavern was Ben Michaels. What a piece of work. There was this gorgeous gal with him, but I haven't figured out yet if it is his wife or just a girl friend. I heard he got married a few years ago, but I don't know if this is the same woman.

Michaels lives in Chicago; I know that much. But exactly what he does is anybody's guess. He never seems to give a straight answer. I talked to him for about an hour and he never once asked me what I was doing or how my life was going. He didn't ask if I was married or had a family. In spite of the fact that I did most of the listening and he did most of the talking, I couldn't quite figure out who he worked for or what he did. He talked a lot about his radio show, but he isn't a disc jockey, and I got the impression that the show had something to do with money, and was mainly a promotional tool for something else that he never quite explained.

Ben was driving an Escalade, but it had Missouri plates, so I am sure it was rented when he flew into KC. I could have given them a ride out to West Plaines from Kansas City since we were driving out at about the same time, but neither of us thought of that. He probably wouldn't have wanted to sit in the car with me for five hours anyway. He probably would not ride in my old Subaru. But there is certainly room in the Escalade for me, since there are only two of them, but he probably didn't know I was still in Lawrence.

Tomorrow is the picnic. It will be interesting to see who is there. Twenty years is a long time. Some people haven't changed a bit and others are hard to recognize. I hope everyone wears name tags.

Ben Michaels

I am glad my ex was able to watch the kids this weekend. This will allow Laura and me some time on the plane and in the car on the way back to my class reunion. We have only been dating three months and I really like Laura.

I feel really blessed that I can provide nice things for myself. Blessed was not a word I said up until a year ago. While my financial advisory business is really going pretty well, I am beginning to realize it's not all my doing.

The problem with West Plaines is it's four hours from any major airport. At least I got us an upgrade to first class from Chicago to Kansas City. First class is the only way to go. We had a blast talking to the couple to the left of us on the plane ride.

I'm a little nervous about my mom officially meeting Laura, especially after my marriage ended in divorce. She really wants us to stay with her, which is what I'm mainly worried about. That is a lot of time together. On the other hand, we won't be there much with the reunion and all.

I did my best to update Laura about some of my classmates, who I hung out with, who I didn't, things like that. Describing what they are doing now, whether they are married, kids, etc.

Laura asked me a tough question on the way there. She said, "Ben, what do you want them to remember about you when you leave Sunday?" I said that I didn't know, but the reality is my answer was pretty shallow. I am actually embarrassed by not having a better answer. I feel successful and am sure my classmates will agree. I also realize this is shallow and this is not enough for me anymore. But knowing something and actually living something are two different things.

We dropped our luggage off at Mom's, got settled and had a great dinner with her. It could not have gone better. I know Mom wanted to like Laura and vice versa. But you never know until it happens.

Our first unofficial class reunion event is meeting at the Town Tavern in West Plaines. The first guy I ran into was Kevin Brown. I was so glad he showed up. We played football together our freshman and sophomore years before I quit. He was a great athlete. I wasn't sure if he'd show up for any of the festivities. I gave him a big man hug, introduced him to Laura, and I met his wife.

Laura and his wife, Sue Ellen, really seemed to hit it off. This seems kind of odd to me. I don't know how to say this, but Kevin's wife looks like a "mom." She has lived in West Plaines all her life and has never really had a career.

Laura looks like – well not like a mom. She's a professional woman who has lived in Chicago for the past 12 years and actually grew up outside of Dallas. Being out of high school 20 years and having God in my life has taught me to look at people on the inside, rather than just the outside.

Kevin Brown

I stopped at the Town Tavern on my way home from work as I do almost every Friday night. Sue Ellen works late at Walmart on Fridays and the kids are at her mom's, so there is never a big hurry to get home anyway.

The usual group was there, plus several that I had not seen for a LONG time. I had almost forgotten that the high school reunion is this weekend and a bunch of people are in for that.

The first person I ran into was Ben Michaels. I didn't know him that well in school, except we played football together for awhile. He always thought he was better than everybody else, even though we all basically grew up together. He doesn't seem to have changed much.

Sue Ellen dropped by the tavern on her way home and I was able to introduce her to Ben and his girlfriend, Laura. She seems real nice. She looked a whole lot more like Chicago than West Plaines, but there is nothing wrong with that. Sue Ellen and Laura had a good time talking like old friends, even though they had just met. Women can do that. In five minutes they can be exchanging recipes, while men are still sniffing each other out.

Anyway, it was fun to see Ben. I am sure I can handle him for a weekend and he won't likely stay around much longer than a few days. For a guy who grew up here, he doesn't seem to fit in with the West Plaines crowd.

While I was talking with Ben and Laura, who should walk in but Gary Davidson? He was sort of the West Plaines resident hippy. Gary is actually a pretty interesting guy. He has had some art shows and I guess he is pretty well known in Lawrence. He is just the opposite of Ben. Ben is sort of a hotshot and Gary is about as down-home as you can get. Ben bought the house a round and Gary kept his hands in his pockets. I got the feeling he was pretty happy that someone else was buying.

Hanging around these guys makes me feel pretty normal. I work with my hands and bring home a paycheck to feed the kids. According to Gary, he is struggling just to pay his bills. And I have no idea what Ben does. He looks like a phony, but I wouldn't know. I'm not around these types very much. I am just happy to go home with Sue Ellen and be with my kids after a hard week of work.

I'm beginning to look forward to the reunion tomorrow. After seeing Gary Davidson and Ben Michaels, I realize that people don't really change much, and this might not be that bad.

Sue Ellen vaguely remembers these guys, but since she was a year behind me, she didn't have much contact with them. I probably won't need to tell her much. She is very perceptive and will be able to figure things out on her own.

Elizabeth Fitzpatrick

Uugh, it is taking forever to get to West Plaines from Denver. Bill was supposed to be home shortly before noon so we could get on the road by 2:00 PM to miss all the Friday afternoon traffic.

He comes rolling in at 2:15, not packed or anything. I had all the kids packed, the dog kenneled and we rolled out of Denver around 3:15 pm. It took us over an hour to get out of Denver and our ETA into West Plaines is now 8:15 PM.

I was really hoping to have dinner with Mom and Dad and then stop down at the local tavern for an informal gathering of my classmates.

Mom said that Dad's prostate cancer is not an aggressive form and they do not plan to do surgery. He'll just take medication to slow down the spread of cancer. That is a relief.

Staying with Mom and Dad is always fun for me, but not for Bill. It gives us a chance for a visit with Mom and Dad. The kids can wake up and talk to their grandparents. Mom always likes to make a big breakfast, and usually at least one of my seven siblings stops in with one of their kids.

Bill was born and raised in Denver and only has one sister. He kind of snubs his nose at our big family in a small town. His favorite saying is: "Eight kids, didn't your folks know what causes that?" Well, our whole family has done quite well for ourselves growing up in this little town. We had to work hard and if we really wanted something, it was up to us to earn the money to pay for it.

Mom is amazing; she still had a full, hot meal ready for us when we arrived. It was great to eat and visit with them. Bill actually did pretty well tonight and he and Dad got to talking about sports and Bill's job.

Dad always did like Bill and sort of lived vicariously through him, career-wise. With Bill being in sales for a major oil company in Denver, he does get to take some great trips and his entertaining budget is quite impressive. I've benefitted from that entertaining budget, too. I am sure we'll talk about some of those trips over the weekend with my classmates.

It is 10:45 PM and Bill has already had 4-5 glasses of wine and I'm tired from packing and the drive. I really need to get the kids to bed shortly, as well. Not sure if it makes sense to meet at the Town Tavern tonight.

I wonder who showed up tonight. I'm sure Ben Michaels is there. He never misses a party. I wonder if Kevin showed up – probably not. I've not seen him since our 10-year reunion and it was only because I saw him and his wife at church. I'm glad Bill is not the jealous type so I can at least talk to Kevin.

You know who just popped in my mind is Gary Davidson. I barely remember him from high school, but we had a pretty good chat at our 10-year reunion. I wonder if he still lives in Lawrence. I have little or no creativity but he does and he's kind of an interesting guy.

Well, my mind is made up. I'm going to stay home tonight and save energy for tomorrow afternoon when we have our classmate picnic down at the park. Then we have the actual class reunion at the VFW center that evening. I'm really getting excited about seeing everyone.

Chapter 2 Discussion Questions:

Has your attitude changed toward any of these
people? Why?

_____

_____

How much do people really change in 10, 20, or 30
years?

_____

_____

How have you changed the most in 10 years?

_____

_____

Chapter 3 – The Picnic

Gary Davidson

It was good to see my mother. She is always encouraging even though I don't think she understands me. She just wants me to be happy, no matter what I am doing. I presume she would like for me to get a regular job, get married, and have some grandkids for her, but she doesn't pry or get pushy. She knows that I have my own priorities, and she knows me well enough not to try to change me.

Mom cooked such a big breakfast I didn't know if I was going to want to eat anything at the picnic. Everybody was supposed to bring a covered dish so she sent a chicken casserole with me. She didn't need to do that; I could have bought something at Casey's on the way.

The first person I saw was Ben Michaels. I figured out that Laura is his girl-friend. Apparently they have just been dating a short time because she doesn't seem to know him real well. I asked her what Ben does and she couldn't really explain it either, so I guess it isn't just me who is confused. He hasn't changed much since high school except that he may be worse. Either that or I had forgotten how egotistical he was. I doubt if Laura will stick around long; she seems really nice, but what do I know about such things. She may be shallow too.

I enjoyed hanging out with Kevin Brown. He seems to have found his soul mate in Sue Ellen, and their two youngest boys are both all boy. I'm not around kids very much, so their energy was sort of overwhelming. Sue Ellen and Kevin don't seem to let anything faze them. I would be exhausted chasing those kids all day.

Kevin was telling me about his job. You wouldn't think that a construction worker and an artist would have that much in common, but we really do. We both like to work with our hands and we can go home at night and point to something that now exists that wasn't there that morning. That is a great feeling. I am glad that I'm not one to push paper or stare at a computer all day.

The only real difference between Kevin and me is that somebody tells him what to make and I have to think it up myself. Some people might say that his work comes from a piece of paper and mine comes from my heart, but I think that is just trying to glorify artists, or maybe rationalize not paying us. I could hardly help but notice that Kevin gets a paycheck every Friday and can feed his family.

There must be some way to work with your hands and heart and still get paid.

The old saying is that a laborer works with his hands; a craftsman works with his hands and head; and an artist works with his hands, head, and heart. That may be true, but that doesn't mean that a craftsman can't put his heart into his work or that an artist can't think. We are a whole lot closer to each other than we think we are. It probably boils down to attitude and intentions.

Kevin wants to build a house that will stand for a hundred years and I want to have a painting hanging in that house for a hundred years. The difference is in the details.

Elizabeth Fitzpatrick joined our conversation. Kevin and Elizabeth dated for awhile in high school and they needed to catch up with their lives. Elizabeth went away to college and never came back. Kevin never left.

Elizabeth's and Kevin's kids are about the same age and quickly became fast friends. It is sort of weird to remember seeing Elizabeth and Kevin cruising around together twenty years ago, and now seeing their children playing together. Life is full of funny little twists and turns.

Kevin seems to have a little inferiority complex about living in West Plaines. He shouldn't. This place isn't all that bad. He has a good life here. I needed to get away to pursue my art, but I now see that I could do it anywhere. In fact, I might be more effective here on the plains away from the distractions and temptations of a place like Lawrence. Lawrence isn't exactly Denver or Chicago, but there is still enough to keep me from my work.

With Mom getting older and Dad gone, I need to think about these things, and I expect I could live a lot cheaper here, too. That is something to think about.

Ben Michaels

Gosh – Laura and I closed down the Town Tavern last night. That was so much fun. Ten years ago we closed it down, too. But this reunion it was more about catching up with some classmates than drinking too much. I like that.

We had another good visit with Mom this morning. I really miss being around her more. It would be great to live in the same city. I don't see her moving to Chicago, though!

I was telling Laura that I wish my two girls were with us for the picnic. I always miss them when I'm gone. They miss me more too, since their mom and I divorced. I am really proud of those two little girls and I know everyone here would love them.

We got to the picnic fashionably late and right away Chris Billings saw me and yelled "MICHAELS"!! I still love it when people yell my name out. He's a cool dude who lives in St. Louis now and works for a huge property and casualty company. He's a VP already and I always knew he would go places. He's the kind of guy you want to impress – not for you, but for him. He brings out the best in everyone. We need to get our families together after the reunion for a long weekend since we are only four hours away by car.

Next we ran into Kevin and Sue Ellen Brown. We had a good time visiting with them last night at the bar. Kevin asked me if I wanted a beer and I said "sure." Kevin was telling me about his motorcycle and how much he loves to ride. I was a little envious of the types of rides he takes. Living in Chicago, I never considered having a bike; too much traffic and too dangerous.

Kevin is one of those guys, the more I spend time with him, the more I like him. He has a "quiet confidence" that I lack. I have more of a "loud confidence," or maybe I'm just loud! Sue Ellen has really grown on me, too. She is one of those women who become more attractive the more you get to know them.

Laura was having a great time, even though she doesn't really know anyone. I do like that about her versus my ex. My ex needed to be "entertained" more, and I never really felt like it was enough. Or maybe it was because it was all about me and less about her. I don't want to make that same mistake again.

I met this guy named Bill who is Elizabeth's husband! He was awesome! I couldn't figure out why Elizabeth didn't come over and talk to us sooner. I thought we always got along pretty well.

Once Elizabeth finally did come over, she and Laura seemed like long-lost friends. I think Elizabeth thought Laura was her type in terms of big city stuff. I even got Elizabeth laughing out loud about some of my stories and jokes. She eased up a lot once she had a beer. She and Bill even asked if we wanted to sit together tonight at the banquet! I know Laura was excited about that, too.

I've always liked that about Elizabeth – she always seemed to know what she wanted. I kind of feel like I've never really known what I wanted (besides to make people laugh and be liked). I have more stumbled into things. Frankly, I want that to change. I want that for my relationship with Laura, my two girls and my career. Maybe Elizabeth can help me with that tonight?

Kevin Brown

Saturday morning.

Today is the day for the high school reunion, but the picnic isn't until 1:00, so I have plenty of time for a ride.

One day I will get a new bike, but for now this old Harley is my best friend; after Sue Ellen, of course. The roar of the pipes is the best sound I can imagine on a crisp morning like this. I'm heading for the lake road to make a quick trip around the lake and back around the Jackson place before heading home for a shower and help Sue Ellen get the kids ready for the reunion.

Out of our class of 125, only about 4 or 5 of us are still in West Plaines. I am sure the ones who left think that we are the losers, like we can't find our way out of town. Maybe they are right. I often wonder why I'm still here. There is really no future here. If you haven't inherited a ranch or a farm, you are pretty much relegated to the bottom of the heap.

Even the ranchers and farmers are struggling, but at least they have roots to keep them here. Often, when I am out on my Hog like this, I think about not turning around. I could be in Denver by dark. But then what?

There is not a week goes by that I don't think about how my life would have been different if I had gone to college. Almost certainly, I would not have come back to West Plaines.

It will be interesting to talk with Elizabeth. We would sometimes talk about the future. She wanted to move to the city and be successful. I don't know what I wanted to do, but I think I was too scared to ever leave this little burg. Maybe that is why we broke up; her ideas were just beyond my comprehension, and she made me nervous when she started talking about new cars and a house in the suburbs.

Sue Ellen has never indicated that she wanted more, but I am never sure that she is happy married to a construction worker. She really deserves more. She loves me and our family, but I am afraid to ask if she has any regrets.

In a few more years the kids will be grown. Will we just keep doing what we are doing until we can draw social security and ….. And what?

Here is the intersection. Left is back to town. Right leads to freedom. Of course, there is no choice, just a fantasy. Who am I kidding? I love Sue Ellen and the kids and I have a good life. Do you suppose that anybody besides me notices that I ride 80 mph out of town and 35 back?

There is my drive. Time to round up the kids. I am sure that Sue Ellen has a nice lunch ready to go for all of us, and probably enough for half the county. She loves cooking and taking care of us. At least she acts like she does. It will be interesting to see what she says about Ben Michaels and some of the other hot shots. That will give me a clue about how she feels about our okay life here in West Plaines.

Elizabeth Fitzpatrick

I'm glad we stayed home last night after getting into West Plaines kind of late. It allowed us to have a nice dinner and visit with Mom and Dad. The kids got settled in and slept in this morning. Bill managed to get 18 holes of golf in with three of my classmates who sent us a text late last night about needing a 4th player. Bill immediately obliged and he's happy now.

Seeing everyone, their spouses and their kids will be fun this afternoon. I'm really proud of my two kids. Melissa is already an accomplished piano player, plays soccer and is a Daisy girl scout. Not bad for a seven year old! Aaron is already playing hockey as a five-year old. Boy, is that an expensive sport! Hey, that's why I make all this money.

We arrived about 2:15 PM. The picnic started at 1:00. Bill managed to have a few drinks during his golf outing. My classmates who golfed with him were feeling no pain either. Bill knows how to have a good time. I'm sure he suggested Bloody Marys or Screwdrivers before they even teed off this morning.

I immediately noticed Bill sitting at a picnic table in the corner where all the booze was. They were laughing with some other classmates "like there was no tomorrow." One of the guys sitting with them was Ben Michaels. He was definitely "holding court" and cracking them up! He has really become handsome over the years – I'd like to catch up with him. Maybe I'll just join their table. There is a really attractive blonde woman sitting with all these guys and it must be Ben's wife or girlfriend. I'm not even sure if he ever married. I'll soon find out.

Before I run over there, I want to say hello to the only guy I dated in high school, Kevin Brown, and his wife Sue Ellen. I knew Bill wouldn't want to talk to them. Bill and I were married at 25, but waited six years before we had kids. It gave us a chance to be a couple and get our careers into high gear. Or at least my career into high gear. Sue Ellen seemed really genuine and in love with Kevin. They have been married 18 years already. Hmm, I can't say I have that spark with Bill like they do. Don't get me wrong, I love him and all.

Speaking of Bill, the last table I stopped at was the table Bill never left. Ben and his girlfriend Laura were still there. I guess Ben was married for nine years and recently divorced. He has a four and two-year old. He and Laura have been dating a few months, but have known each other for 15 years. Ben still has the gift of gab, except he's funnier now. I thought Laura rocked. We hit it off right away. She and Ben live in Chicago and Laura is very cosmopolitan. We've already made plans to sit together at the class reunion banquet tonight. I'm getting really excited about this evening!

Chapter 3 discussion questions:

How do you unwind?

_____

_____

What would have been your experience, had you been at the picnic?

_____

_____

Discuss a time you wanted to just "ride out of town and never come back?"

_____

_____

Chapter 4 – That Evening

Gary Davidson

Kevin said something at the picnic that got me
thinking. He said he had been out tending his
garden on his Harley. That was such a funny thing
to say so I asked him what he meant. He said his
mind was a garden that needed tending. The more I
think about it, the truer that sounds. I presume that
when we are born that our minds are like an empty
lot which has been fertilized and sown with various
combinations of seeds. As we mature, the plants
grow and can easily become overgrown with weeds.

I told Kevin that maybe we are all given different
amounts of fertilizer, or basic intelligence, and we
have a variety of seeds or gifts or talents. It is how
we nurture those seeds, tend to the weeds, and make
the most out of the intelligence that we have that
makes all the difference. He said his soil wasn't
very good so he had to work hard. I don't know if
he was joking or if he was serious, but he had a
good point.

I was born with all these artistic seeds and I feel like
the weeds are strangling them. The problem is, I can
hardly tell which ones are the weeds, and I don't

want to pull up perfectly good plants. Obviously, smoking pot is weeds; we even call it that. Since I can quit any time I want, I probably should. But how about the other stuff: my friends, the music I listen to, the stupid TV shows I watch. Are these things choking out the good stuff or are these things the good stuff? I sure wish I knew a good way to tell.

I mentioned this to my mom when I got back to her house and she showed me a drawing of her garden with marks and sketches where the various vegetables and flowers are planted. She said she has no trouble telling when something is in the wrong place because she has the plot all laid out. After all, a weed is a perfectly good plant. It is just in the wrong place at the wrong time.

Wow. So I need to draw up a plan of what I want my life to look like, determine what seeds I have and start pruning and watering to make it happen. That may sound easy, but I have no idea where to start, and I certainly have no idea what my mind, or my life, or even my garden should look like. And besides, what if it doesn't work out? Aren't I just setting myself up for failure?

I wonder how many of my classmates have a plan or even a sketchy garden plot of what they want their life to look like? And if so, are things going according to the plan.

A garden is a living, growing thing, and plans can change. Different plants bloom or produce fruit at different times and on different cycles, so it is not a one-time or one-plan-fits-all kind of thing.

I wanted to talk with Kevin about this some more at the VFW, but there was little time for talking. With the speeches, loud music, and people half drunk, it was not a good time to talk philosophy. I was reminded one more time about how different we all are.

Michaels was the rep from our class, so he got to speak. I don't know what the subject was supposed to be, but he mainly told jokes and reminded us that he was the cool guy in our class. I still am not sure if he even remembers me, even though we were in several classes together, and I have already seen him three times this weekend.

Another funny thing happened at the VFW. Elizabeth Fitzpatrick said that she had a painting by a Santa Fe artist who had the same name as me. I had her describe it and I realized that it was one of mine! She thought the artist was from Santa Fe because she bought the painting when they were there on vacation. When I told her that that was me, she just stared at me in disbelief. I still don't know if she believed me. Gary Davidson is a pretty common name.

On Monday I am driving to Santa Fe. I can't wait to tell Carol, the gallery owner, that story. There are probably a lot of stories like that in the art world. People just can't believe that somebody they know, or grew up with, is selling art in a gallery. Maybe that will encourage Carol to push my stuff more. I sure could use the jack.

Kevin invited me to join him and Sue Ellen for lunch tomorrow. He said he wanted to talk some more about that garden. I think he was referring to his life and not his real garden, but I am not sure. If he gives me a sack of zucchinis, that will be okay, too.

Ben Michaels

It is so great to be back in West Plaines this weekend. I haven't laughed this hard in a long time. Laura commented about that. She said "I've never heard you laugh from the gut like that."

After an hour power nap, Laura and I sat with Mom and got her laughing about the stories from the picnic. I really do love to make people laugh – so much that I forget to laugh myself sometimes.

When we were driving to the VFW hall in West Plaines, I asked Laura if she wanted to make a few "mains." She said, " what is that?" So I showed her! It's when you drive up and down the same street (Main Street) and wave and honk at your friends. Seems weird - we would do this for hours in high school and even when I'd come back from the university on weekends.

We drove past the old auditorium where we used to meet people driving Main to make plans where we were going next. I took her past the old meat packing plant and the grocery store where I worked after school and on weekends. Life was a lot simpler back then – albeit boring in some ways.

When we arrived at the VFW Hall, it brought back memories of wedding receptions and family gatherings. When we walked in, it smelled exactly the way I remembered it – good food with an "old building" smell. It was nostalgic for me.

Elizabeth and Bill were there early to save a table for a bunch of us. She yelled over at Laura (instead of me) to join them. After we put our belongings down, I went to Elizabeth and asked if I could get some advice from her this evening about my life/career, etc. She had a shocked yet honored look on her face. Now the question is when? We are leaving tomorrow around noon.

There were still 45 minutes of the social hour, so Laura and I went to get a drink. Bud Light, Bud, wine in a box, sweet and sour were our choices. Laura asked me what a sweet and a sour was. We both laughed when I told her – it's either 7-Up or Squirt with whiskey. She went with the Bud Light.

Laura went over and sat with Elizabeth while I talked with Bill at the bar. Bill seems like a great guy. Within a few minutes, I realized he's not really happy in his marriage. I personally have become more spiritual the past year since my first wife and I split up. I really see how I contributed to that divorce. Unfortunately, I realized this too late to do anything about it.

Next thing I know, I'm giving Bill advice about his marriage. I asked him on a scale of 1-10 (1 is low and 10 is high) how happy he is in his marriage. He said a 6.5. When I asked him about Elizabeth, he said "I don't know." I could tell he wasn't sure he wanted to know.

I didn't want to know a year ago either. On the other hand, I didn't want to be at my 20-year class reunion - recently divorced.

Bill thanked me for being real with him. He said he never had another guy give him good advice like this. He made reference to his drinking. Saying it takes the edge off his relationship with Elizabeth.

He never feels like he is good enough around her. He's not sure whether she needs him in her life. She is so capable in many areas. I guess I never thought about that before. How important it is to need each other in the marriage…as opposed to being independent.

Once we were seated, Kevin and Sue Ellen sat next to us. We were sitting across from Elizabeth and Bill. Also, Gary Davidson sat next to Bill. I hadn't seen him in 10 years – or at least I thought. I was a little embarrassed because he said he was at the Town Tavern and the picnic this afternoon. Just between you and me – I have no recollection of that. He laughed and said "some things never change." I kind of get the feeling that it was not funny to him.

The banquet was long – they honored all the classes present. It took forever for them to get to our class because they did all the old people first. Elizabeth told me that no one from our class had offered to be our spokesperson and asked if I would do it. Heck yea!

I went up to the podium and told the entire group a little about myself and where I "hail from," and then just started telling a few stories. Next thing I know, not only are my classmates laughing, but the whole VFW Hall! I saw this 88-year-old guy – been out of high school for 70 years cracking up! I totally loved it. I really think I have a talent when it comes to this. My dream is to be "Famous Funny." Is it too late for me at age 38? I wonder if Elizabeth can help me sort through all this.

Kevin Brown

I told Gary my theory about my brain being a garden that needs tending. I was thinking about how I felt like my garden looks after a good rain with all those weeds and thistles choking out the good things in life. He quickly started talking about fertilizer and seeds and garden plots. I was talking about being confused a lot and needing to ride to let my brains air out. When he equated intelligence with fertilizer, I told him I had poor soil so I had to work hard. He just laughed.

That was an off-hand comment, but it may be true, especially the seeds part. There are so many different kinds of people at this reunion, it is hard to believe that we all grew up in the same little town and drank the same water. I guess we did all start out with different packs of seeds in our heads.

Elizabeth is smart, a hard charger, and is successful in Denver. I am none of those things. We grew up together and our parents were friends. Obviously, we were given a different pack of seeds.

If Elizabeth and I had gotten married, we would have made each other miserable. We are so much different. I am still intimidated by her, and I am not sure that her husband, Bill, isn't just a little bit intimidated by her as well. She isn't trying to be intimidating. In fact, she goes out of her way to be nice, but there is just something about her that says she has it together. I am glad that Sue Ellen and I have each other. Neither of us can get by without the other. That may be what marriage is all about...needing each other.

And I have no idea where Michaels came from. At the banquet at the VFW he got up and started talking about how great his life was and telling funny stories. He *was* funny, but hey, he was there with a girlfriend, not his wife. He had already messed up one marriage, and he was trying to convince us how cool he was.

If it goes back to what seeds we were given, what gifts and talents we have, our interest, or how we were made, then we need to cut each other some slack. We shouldn't expect others to be like us, and more importantly, not kick ourselves because we can't be like somebody else.

I wonder what they say about me. Do they feel sorry for me because I never made it out of West Plaines, or do they think I am just boring with a wife and three kids, one of whom is about to graduate himself.

What seeds was I given anyway? I never really thought about that before. I like to work with my hands. Is that a seed? I like to go home tired at night, knowing that I have accomplished something. Is that some sort of seed? What other seeds do I have and what would a perfectly groomed garden of my life look like? Should a guy with poor soil like me even be thinking about such things? Shouldn't this be left to the preachers and philosophers?

I am looking forward to asking Gary more about this at lunch tomorrow. He probably has it well thought out. He seems to be a guy who does a lot of thinking, at least when he is off the weed. He said he was driving down to Santa Fe to visit an art gallery that has sold some of his paintings. If I didn't have to work, I think I would go with him. He is a neat guy once you get him talking. Also, I wonder if I could make something that would sell as art. I have wood-working skills and I always wanted to try some woodcarving or something. You never know, maybe I have some seeds back there that haven't sprouted yet.

Elizabeth Fitzpatrick

I was so excited to sit with Laura tonight. I really
like her. I figured we better get to the VFW Hall a
little early to save seats for her, Ben and us. Bill
wanted to take a nap after the picnic and I told him
no way. I had to get ready and he needed to help
with the kids. My parents already had been
watching the kids most of the day.

Bill really frustrates me sometimes. The only way I
could talk him into getting to the reunion early was
to remind him that the social hour started at 6:00.
Manipulation - I need to do what I need to do.

On the way to the VFW Hall, suddenly Bill wants
me to tell him more about West Plaines. I'm like,
"what are you talking about and why now?" He has
historically made fun of my upbringing, big family,
etc, since he was born and raised in Denver. He said
this weekend was the most fun he's ever had in
West Plaines. So I asked what the difference was –
and he said "Ben Michaels." I like Ben, but that's
been the best part? Amazing!

So we get to the VFW at 6 PM sharp. I grab the
table while Bill heads straight to the bar. I'm like,

"could you wait a minute?" Next thing I know, he's laughing with the two volunteer bartenders, so I go over to find out why. I was a little embarrassed by him asking for all these different mixed drinks that he knows they don't know how to make.

Around 6:15, Ben and Laura arrived and I let Laura know where we are sitting right away. She came over and sat with me and we yakked it up. One thing that really struck me about Laura is her unconditional love for Ben. She is so laid back – yet has such a presence about her. It's a little bewildering to me. I've always thought - to have a presence - you need to be bolder about it. Hers is more subtle. There must be some middle ground there for me.

She and Ben have that "young love" piece to their relationship. Bill and I have lost that. Not sure we ever had it to the extent they have it. I just knew I wanted to get married and have a family. Bill was a good guy, in my midst, and he wanted to marry me. Done deal!

I looked up and Ben and Bill are joining us. After Ben gave me a hug, he asked if he could talk to me about some career stuff. At first, I thought he was kidding and just wanted to crack a joke. But then I realized he was serious. I was a little flattered. This conversation will be interesting.

Then Kevin and Sue Ellen joined us and Gary Davidson. Gary sat by me and I am so glad he did. He's so much more interesting than I remember. In fact, I bought a beautiful art piece in Santa Fe two years ago by an artist with his last name. It didn't hit me until tonight that I had a classmate with that name.

Then he drops the bomb – it was his painting! I'm not 100% sure he was telling the truth, but I really think he was. How cool is that?

Everyone was telling me that we didn't have a spokesperson for our class. While I could have done it, I get tired of "taking care of everything," so I asked Michaels – and he's all in. Great – I was off the hook.

I must say he did a fantastic job – everyone was laughing. Well, almost everyone – except Gary. He was muttering something under his breath – I couldn't really hear what he was saying, but just nodded my head. Not sure what that was all about.

Well – the banquet was almost over and I hadn't had a chance to talk to Ben yet. Maybe, we can all go somewhere after this and I'll see what he had in mind.

Chapter 4 discussion questions:

What kind of seeds are in your garden?

_____

_____

How do you plan to cultivate your mind?

_____

_____

What area of your life do you have serious interests that need to be developed?

_____

_____

Chapter 5 – 10 PM

Gary Davidson

After the dinner at the VFW, I decided to stop by the tavern. That seemed like where everybody was headed.

I was able to strike up a conversation with Elizabeth. I was still curious about why she bought my painting. As we talked, I realized that the things that she liked about it, the colors, how it looked in her house, the size, and the type of frame, were all things that were of only minor interest to me. Yet she loved the painting and paid good money for it. Interesting...

I also got the feeling that I wasn't the sort of person who she would normally be talking to in a bar. In fact, she was quite amused with the whole situation. Her non-verbal language said something like, "Look at me, talking to a person like this, in a place like this." I am sure that I am not the type of person in her normal circle of friends. I will probably be a topic of conversation when she gets home. I can hear it now: "There was this old hippy in my class who is an artist, and I already own a piece of his art, and I didn't even know it."

But that got me thinking. If she had seen me at an art fair, would she have bought my painting? Is it possible that my appearance or persona is a barrier to my financial success? My friends can't afford my work, and the people who can aren't my friends. One solution is to rely more on galleries as the middleman, or maybe I could think more about how people perceive me.

Would buying some new clothes and getting a hair cut be perceived as selling out, or would it just be good business? And what is the difference between the two anyway? I can't see myself joining the Chamber of Commerce, but what I am doing now isn't working. I would probably be the only artist there. Would that be smart or just weird?

Getting away from my artsy friends in Lawrence and getting some new perspective has been good for my head. In some ways, we are the pretentious ones. Looking down on Kevin who never left town, or the uppity people like Elizabeth who we consider uncultured, but make all the money.

And then there is Ben. What can you say about somebody who everybody likes, but nobody really likes? Is that even possible? The "life of the party" with no friends. Obviously there is more to this story than meets the eye. It reminds me of my friend Kyle who committed suicide. I loved Kyle, as did everybody else who knew him. He just didn't love himself all that much and decided to end it all. It goes to show that things aren't always as they seem. I have to think about Ben more. I think he has a high need for friends but doesn't know how to go about developing them and ends up pushing everybody away in the process.

Lunch with Kevin, Sue Ellen, and the boys was fun. Kevin seems to share in the whole town's inferiority complex, but overall, I think he is content. He has found his place, even if he doesn't know it. Neither he nor Sue Ellen is particularly ambitious, but seem to feel guilty about not being so. Our society puts pressure on people to achieve and teaches us that that is the road to happiness. The problem is: what if you are already happy? Do we have to keep on striving for more or can we just be happy where we are? I think the pressure to achieve is what makes us unhappy.

Am I happy, and if not, what would it take? Do I need more money? If so, how much? Maybe just a little bit more. Would more people praising my work make me happy? Probably. How about more friends or a wife and family? Maybe happiness is just an attitude that is not really dependent on external things but comes from inside. Actually, that is joy. Happiness has to do with what is happening now, or at least, our perception of what is happening. But that too, is an attitude. It is time to start thinking about these things and drawing up a garden plot for my life, so I will know what to cultivate and what are the weeds.

This is weird, but I am really looking forward to seeing Carol in Santa Fe. We have only met a couple of times and she has sold several of my pieces in her gallery, but she seems to live comfortably in two worlds and moves freely between the two.

She is able to communicate and relate to business and society people like Elizabeth, and at the same time have a good understanding of artists like me. I expect that she doesn't switch personalities, but rather has an ability to be the same all the time and connect with a wide range of people in the process. I would like to be able to do that.

Ben Michaels

So after we left the VFW Hall and I've got everyone coming to the Town Tavern for more laughs. I saw Elizabeth walking ahead of me. After my little "performance" at the banquet, I ran up to her to make sure to meet me at the bar.

I ran into two of my cousins when I first walked in and started talking to them. The conversation got boring pretty quick and then I caught Elizabeth out of the corner of my eye. I excused myself and made a beeline to her. Gary Davidson was there and as soon as I walked up – I could tell he hated me. What is up with that? Anyway, he left and Elizabeth and I started talking. Or should I say – I started talking.

Not sure what came over me, but I rambled on and on for about fifteen minutes. Since I have found God, I really attempt to be more of a giver than a taker. Laura is a perfect example of that for me. She is totally different than my first wife. I was a taker back then and I married a taker. Now I'm a giver and am dating a giver. It's a totally different relationship.

So after I "vomited words" all over Elizabeth, I noticed she was a little irritated. I thought: Oh great now I've messed this up. But then she asked me a zinger question. She said: "Ben, what do you really want for your life?" Her question stopped me in my tracks. She kind of had a stern look on her face, but I realized that was the question I had not asked myself.

My whole life I have been running. What am I running to OR what am I running from? Along the way, I've had some success, but it never leads to what I really want. Something always seems to be missing. It's insatiable.

God has filled part of that hole for me. The other part - I haven't let Him in yet. So I stare at Elizabeth some more and then I mutter "To be an international, transformational television talk show host." After I said it, I thought – where did that come from? And then thought - that was really good! The look on Elizabeth's face verified that it was really good.

So then she asked, "on what topics?" Again, I mutter out God, divorced Dad's, and relationships. This is so weird. The only thing I could think was: even though I thought I was a long way from knowing what I wanted, I was really closer than I thought.

I started to get misty eyed after we started talking. So I know this is what I'm supposed to do. Then Elizabeth asked if we wanted to talk after the reunion about the plan to accomplish all this. I was so thankful to God because that's why I have been so drawn to her this weekend. She is a planner and an implementer. All the opposite things I am.

When I told her about my weekly radio program in Chicago, I could tell she was genuinely impressed. I think this is the first time I have felt impressive to Elizabeth. The interesting part is: I don't need her approval like I used to.

After we were done talking, I looked for Gary Davidson to find out if I had offended him. But he was nowhere to be found. I think I'll call him once I get back to Chicago. It's obvious I have done something to offend him. At this point in my life, I'm attempting to make amends for my past. And Gary is part of that past.

Kevin Brown

Gary came by for lunch before he headed out of town. He was driving an old Subaru which I hope makes it to Santa Fe. I guess he has been driving it for years so he has confidence in it like an old friend. There aren't many Subarus in West Plaines. The primo choice is the Ford F-250, but Chevy Silverados and Dodge Rams have their followers.

My choice is whichever one I can get the best deal on. The Ford dealer is a good friend and wants me to stay loyal to the brand, so my last three trucks have been Fords. The three topics of conversation that we avoid at the tavern are politics, religion, and what brand of trucks are the best. Come to think of it, aren't these all about the same thing? I know the separation between trucks and religion is pretty narrow.

Gary was still talking about cultivating his garden and trying to figure out life in general. He asked me if I was happy. Happy? I guess I am, but then my old classmates come back from places like Chicago and Denver and I begin to think that I am a loser, having never left West Plaines.

I have no desire to live in one of those places. Driving to Wichita for the weekend is a big deal for me, and I am always happy to get home – so maybe I am happy here. I don't know anything different.

I would like to make more money, but who wouldn't? I get by and my kids have three meals a day and our utilities are paid. Should I be doing something more?

Gary said that he didn't want to look back on his life when he gets old and have regrets about what could have been. Maybe that is the secret. When I look back on my life fifty years from now, will I regret having done some of the things I've done, or worse, regret not doing the things I didn't do? The truth is: I don't know what it would be. I love my wife and family and I enjoy my work. Is there supposed to be something else?

If there is, perhaps it is reaching outside my family to helping others. In talking with my classmates this weekend, I didn't hear many people talking about what they were doing to build their community or reach out to other people who might need help. I'm no different. I go to work and come home, sleep, and go to work again. My work helps people, but is that enough?

I heard some of the guys last week talking about Habit for Humanity coming to town to build a couple of houses. They were looking for volunteers. My first thought was if I am going to be swinging a hammer, I had better be getting paid. But as I think about it, I am not so sure. After all, building is what I know. It is not like I would be competing against myself, because these are houses that wouldn't get built any other way, and this town sure needs this sort of thing. I think I will call around next week and see what they need. I am ready to branch out a little bit and this is as good a place to start as any.

Elizabeth Fitzpatrick

I have to say the reunion was more fun than I expected. It's really weird that Ben and Laura are the reason Bill and I had more fun. I've been thinking about that a lot tonight. Part of it is the history that Ben and I share. I have known of Ben since 1st grade. That's 32 years! But I never really knew him.

On the other hand, I just met Laura this weekend and Bill just met Ben this weekend and we hit it off so quickly.

When I think about my Denver friends, they tend to be more superficial. They are really talented and polished like Laura. But they are not as genuine and unconditional. That's the word that keeps coming up for me with Laura. Actually, I feel the same way about Kevin and Sue Ellen. They unconditionally love people. I need to be more like that with Bill. I'm nice to him when he fits my mold for how things need to be. When he doesn't fit that mold, I'm angry with him. That is not really fair to him – or me.

So we are walking from the VFW Hall to the Town Tavern. Ben came running up to me on the sidewalk and said – "hey I really want to talk to you and I'll meet you at the bar." And off he went grabbing another classmate and putting him in a head lock. Some things never change.

I ran into my brother Jim at the bar and while we were talking, Gary Davidson walked up. He was just kind of standing there looking at us, so I introduced him to my brother. I was a little distracted because I wanted to talk to Jim more, but then he needed get back to his wife. So Gary and I started talking. I may have come off a little rude to Gary because he interrupted my brother and my conversation.

Once we started visiting more, I was convinced it was his artwork that I bought in Santa Fe. I told him that really meant a lot to me. Besides, it looks fabulous in our great room. I was a little embarrassed that I wasn't more articulate about why I liked his artwork.

I told him how Carol in Santa Fe and I met. We were sorority sisters at the University of Colorado. The thought occurred to me that she is single and so is Gary. They have art in common and I wondered if there was any other history between them. As I looked at Gary - as a 38-year-old man as opposed to an 18-year-old hippie – I realized he's a pretty nice looking guy. He just needs an "Extreme Makeover."

There I go again being conditional about things! At least I was able to see past his appearance to who Gary is. Maybe I'm growing more than I think?

Then Ben came up and Gary's body language was so obvious that he doesn't like Ben. Ben of course didn't notice and said – "Can we talk now?" I looked at Gary to make sure that was okay and he just excused himself and left. Even Ben noticed that.

Then Ben did a "brain dump" on me. He told me about how he found God after his divorce a year ago. That he started a new financial planning business and loves it. Yet feels like something is missing is his new business. After about 15 minutes of him talking, I just asked him the question: "Ben – what do you really want out of life"? He said, "I want to be an international, transformational television talk show host who talks about God, divorced dads, and relationships!" After he said that, I was asking myself why I can't articulate what I really want.

Then he told me about the radio show he has been doing in Chicago. His eyes totally lit up. I can totally see him doing that and that explains why he commanded the room so quickly tonight at the reunion.

Not sure why I did this, but I offered to visit with him by phone after we all get home and see if I can help him put some "teeth" into his dreams. Of course, I know I am able to help him. The question is – can Ben help himself?

Chapter 5 discussion questions:

How important is it to be able to articulate what you want from life? What are your thoughts about having it in writing?

_____

_____

What if things don't go according to the plan?

_____

_____

Do successful people have written goals or do people with written goals become successful?

_____

_____

Chapter 6 - Leaving West Plaines

Gary Davidson

Santa Fe is beautiful. As I drive around town I realize why so many artists have settled here. The light is gorgeous and everywhere you look there is something that makes you want to get out a canvas and paint.

I need to be thinking about moving somewhere else. I grew up in West Plaines and then went to Lawrence to school. I am still there twenty years later. I consider myself a creative person, but I have never lived outside of Kansas and seldom even travel outside the state. I am a lot more boring than I think I am, or would like to be.

I met Carol at the gallery and she is a lot prettier and friendlier than I had remembered. We had only met over business at art shows, so I was surprised when she asked me over to her house for dinner. Like me, she has never married and has devoted her life to art. I love making art, but she enjoys sharing all kinds of art with her clients through her gallery. She has a small stable of artists, like me, who supply her gallery with a huge variety of works.

I expected that we would be talking about what art she wanted to show, but instead she wanted to know what was on my mind. I told her about the idea of our mind being a garden with our giftedness being seeds and our intelligence being the fertilizer. When I told her that our choices in life are how we cultivate the garden and we can destroy the seedlings as they come up, or we can tend to them until they are strong and beautiful. The choices we make along the way will determine what our garden looks like even though the seeds and richness of the soil were determined a long time ago.

Carol asked how my garden was coming and I said that I couldn't tell the weeds from the vegetables, and as near as I could tell the weeds were doing fine. She reminded me my art definitely indicates I had some good seeds in there. I need to look for some more good plants. I suppose that I thought that one good seed was enough, but one nice plant doesn't make a garden any more than one good painting makes an artist or a gallery.

Ben Michaels

Mom cooked us a great brunch before we took off around 12:30 PM. I miss Mom so much. I wish she would find a companion. She would be a great catch for some guy. I know the divorce from Dad 24 years ago just ripped her heart out. So much baggage there.

Laura and I threw all our stuff in the rented Escalade and took one more spin down Main Street honking our horn – making sure they knew the "celebrities" were leaving – ha! We saw Kevin parked outside the coffee shop and told him good bye and to keep up the good work helping West Plaines grow.

Then off we went. Laura held my hand and thanked me for bringing her to West Plaines and how much she enjoyed it. Man, I don't deserve someone like her. Total opposite of how my ex used to describe West Plaines.

I cannot wait to see my girls! As they are getting older now (4 and 2), they realize more when I'm gone. My older one cried last night when I called them because she missed me. Wow, that's a great feeling. I need to better plan how to involve my girls in my life more and in Laura's. With me having joint custody, I've been more reactive than proactive in how I spend time with them.

Maybe Elizabeth can help me with goal setting there, too. I am definitely calling her once I get back to Chicago. I've promised too many things in the past and not followed through. Now more than ever, I need to follow through. I need to follow through in many areas of my life.

Elizabeth Fitzpatrick

Uuuggghh – I am so tired this morning. Mom and Dad invited my local sibling Jim and his family over for brunch before we drove back to Denver. Jim and his wife Janet were at the bar last night. They have two boys who are already teenagers and I really miss Jim and his family.

Bill was really helpful this morning as we were getting the kids packed up prior to my family arriving. Once we sat down and began having brunch, the topic of conversation turned to my reunion. Bill and I both lit up about how much fun we had.

My brother Jim brought up the conversation about Gary Davidson and asked what he was doing these days. Everyone in the dining room cracked up when they heard I "accidently" bought one of his paintings in Santa Fe. They were also impressed Gary had done so well for himself.

Speaking of "cracking up," Jim's wife, Janet, said she ran into Ben Michaels at the Town Tavern last night. She went on and on about what a great guy he's become. Of course, Bill jumped in right away that he's never had so much fun in West Plaines – and much of it had to do with Ben and his girlfriend Laura. At first I was a little uncomfortable that so many people like Ben now. To make myself feel better, I told them Ben had confided in me that he wanted my help in pursuing dreams for his life. My mom right away jumped in that she thought I'd be great at that.

I am great at that, so why am I uncomfortable with helping Ben? Am I such a small person that it would bother me if Ben "surpassed" me career wise?

After we finished brunch, we packed all our belongings into our SUV, said our goodbyes and were on our way back to Denver.

I fell asleep 15 minutes outside of West Plaines while Bill drove. I woke up at the Colorado border because the kids always get excited when we enter a new state – especially Colorado! Bill asked if I could drive for awhile. He, too, fell asleep rather quickly and I started to reminisce about the whole weekend.

It really was a ton of fun. I'm so glad I have a place to go back to – that I can call home. It reminded me I really need to do a better job of staying in contact with certain classmates. While 10 years goes by pretty quickly, I don't want to wait until I'm age 48 to visit with some of them again.

Was I supposed to call Ben or vice versa? Well, knowing Ben, a couple of weeks will go by and he'll have already forgotten we talked about this. Once again, I'll have to make the first move to get things started.

Aaahhh – I see the mountains and can see some of the downtown skyscrapers. We are about 45 minutes from home. I can't wait to get to my beautiful home, my own bed, and get back to work. While I've had great three-day weekend, I'm eager to get back to a routine. Oh and I need to take a much better look at Gary's artwork. I also need to call Carol in Santa Fe and have a good laugh. In fact, I think Gary is driving directly from West Plaines to Santa Fe. He'll probably get there tonight or tomorrow!

Kevin Brown

This weekend has got me thinking. I really have it pretty good here. West Plaines isn't such a bad place and mainly, it suits me. This is what I know and it is a good fit for me and my family.

I am definitely going to check into this Habitat for Humanity deal, and I need to start thinking about making this town a better place for my family and our friends. At 38, I am no longer a kid. I am beginning to see this town is "us." People my age who are still here need to step up and make this town a better place. It needs to be a place that people like Ben, Elizabeth and Gary don't have to leave to do what they want to do.

Chapter 6 discussion questions:

Of the places you have lived, where was your favorite place?

_____

_____

Are you living in your favorite place now? What about your surroundings makes it great?

_____

_____

If money was not an object, in what city & state do you believe you were intended to bloom?

_____

_____

Chapter 7

TEN YEARS LATER

Gary Davidson

Well, you guessed it. I never left Santa Fe. I went back to Lawrence, rented a U-Haul and moved all my stuff to Santa Fe. I rented a little house not far from Carol's gallery. The next year we got married and I moved into her house.

I like to kid her that she has become my slave driver. She insists that I paint eight hours a day and gets very upset if I smoke a joint. She says I am a professional artist and need to act like it. I love it! I need somebody to keep telling me this and make me do what I love to do anyway. In Lawrence, it was too easy to hang out or get stoned and never make a real effort to make great art. At the gallery, I can see peoples reactions and hear their comments and it helps me grow as an artist. I think most artists underestimate the value of feedback. To make art that people want to buy is not selling out. Sales are just a validation of the quality of the art, or "product," as Carol calls it. I pour out my blood on a piece of canvas and she calls it a product. That's why we need each other, I guess. We balance out to reality.

She lets me paint whatever I want, and as soon as she sees a new piece, she has a list of clients in mind to call. She is selling my art as fast as I can paint it. Is this an artist's dream or what? I wonder how many of the famous artists of the past had a wife telling them to get back in that studio and paint. A funny thought, but it's probably not far from the truth.

I am not doing as many art shows as I was. Since I am the featured artist at the gallery, I keep busy just supplying that. I don't want to become a painting factory like Thomas Kincaid, but I think Carol would like for the gallery to be exclusively my work. After all, 100% of the sale is better than a commission on somebody else's stuff, and I am the biggest seller there already.

Carol was hesitant about leaving the gallery for a long weekend in the tourist season, but I am glad she decided to come. She remembers Elizabeth from her college days and sees her at sorority events sometimes, so that will be fun for her.

I have heard about all the changes in West Plaines and am eager to see if they are really improvements or just new. I hope the town hasn't lost the small-town charm it had when I was growing up.

Sometimes these little towns think they are really making progress when they tear down the 100-year-old buildings and put up a McDonalds. I will withhold judgment until I see it and talk to some of the locals about what has happened. I heard Kevin Brown is on the city council, so it will be interesting to see what they have to say.

Sue Ellen Brown

I am still stunned. They say it takes a year to recover and it has only been three months. Kevin's high school reunion is this weekend and I am sure many of his classmates haven't heard yet.

Kevin was out for his usual Saturday morning ride when George Lewis pulled out right in front of him in his pickup truck. There was no place to go when Kevin hit the truck. He died two hours later at the hospital of massive head injuries.

The last ten years of Kevin's life really brought him out of his shell. Ever since his 20-year reunion, he had found a new love for this town.

That tornado a few years back really wrecked havoc, but it was a blessing in disguise for us and the other builders around here. A lot of towns shrivel up and die after something like this, but we were excited about rebuilding and getting rid of some of those old buildings that had been an eye sore for decades.

The Town Tavern is gone and in its place is a nice new family-style restaurant. I think some of the guys who used to stop at the tavern on the way home for work, now stop at the new place for breakfast. That is a big change. And since some of them, Kevin included, got elected to the city council, we can actually make some legitimate changes around here.

The "young" guys, (well, they are a lot younger that the old guys who were on the city council) had just begun updating this place when the tornado hit. That gave them an opportunity to set some new zoning standards and building codes.

The higher standards benefited us because Kevin always insisted on high quality work. The new codes keep out a lot of sloppy contractors. We were able to get some federal funding to rebuild and the new buildings encouraged some of the locals to follow their dreams by opening new shops and boutiques downtown.

There is even an antique row with a half dozen antique shops on First Street. This brings a lot of traffic off the highway with out-of-towners looking for "country fresh" merchandise. Of course, the antique dealers buy their stuff in the city, but that's the way things work. The antique shoppers have lunch at the new restaurant, so this town is really prospering, at least by West Plaines standards.

A couple people from Applebee's were in town last week scouting locations. I don't know if that would be a good thing or not, but I really think that we are about to the point where we could support a major chain restaurant like that. And if Applebee's gives us the nod, other chains might follow.

I am sure that Kevin would have been excited for Ben, Elizabeth, Gary and all the rest to see what we have done with their old town. I think they will be impressed. But even if they are not, it pleases me to see what Kevin and the guys have been able to accomplish, and I know it will be a great place for our grandkids to grow up.

Ben Michaels

We've had a great drive so far. Ten years ago, I would never have considered driving to West Plaines from Chicago. My girls have had a blast stopping at the "Field of Dreams" farmstead in Iowa. We've stayed at some great bed and breakfasts along the way, went to a really cool zoo in Omaha, and attended a Royals baseball game in

Kansas City last night. Only 84 miles to West Plaines.

I used to think first class airfare was the only way to go. Don't get me wrong, I still love to fly first class, but you can't put a price on spending good quality time with your family. I would have never done this before marrying Laura. We will celebrate our 10th anniversary this December. I am so grateful this marriage has not only lasted, but flourished.

As I was driving to my 20-year reunion 10 years ago in a rented Escalade after Laura and I flew into Kansas City – I really wanted to impress everyone. The funny thing is, I am still driving into West Plaines in an Escalade, but it's 3 years old, it's mine, paid for, and I really don't care what my classmates think! Well, maybe a little.

I'm a little nervous about coming back to the reunion. Mom called about three months ago about Kevin Brown's death in a motorcycle accident. I know he loved that bike. It was the first nice day in March and I am sure Kevin was itching to get on his bike.

Laura made the comment how strong Sue Ellen and Kevin's marriage seemed when we saw them last 10 years ago. I am sure Sue Ellen is really struggling. Kevin's death really got to Laura and me. Made us appreciate each other and what God is doing in our lives even more.

I've got so much to catch up with my classmates about: first and foremost, the love of my life - Laura. My daughters are 14 and 12 now and I am so happy with how they have matured – considering they came from a broken home. Even my relationship with my ex is pretty good. I need to give that credit to Laura – and God.

My divorce 11 years ago brought me to my knees. It really forced me to decide what was working for me and not working for me. I sought God because I knew I was out of my league in fixing the mess I was in. I worked on being the best single guy I could be – and then Laura walked into my life. I don't think that was an accident. Nor do I think she would have been interested in the old me – but she saw the new me – even before I did! I remember Elizabeth saying how she loved how Laura was so unconditional – and she was right.

Speaking of Elizabeth – I have not talked to her in about 4 years, but she really did help me get clear on what I wanted for my life. I remember the day, almost 10 years ago, when she point blank asked me, "Why are you in the financial advisory business – it seems to be getting in the way of what you really want!" She was right, one more area of my life where I had gotten complacent and comfortable.

Of course her counsel - and a lot of trust and faith-led to the television show I've been hosting the past two years in Chicago called the "Happy Husband." I was created to do this! I came from a broken home, got divorced myself, and now realize as the leader of my family the influence I have in my family and ultimately for my happiness. Ten years ago, who would have thought? I still get to be the "performer" I've always wanted to be – yet what I do is having a huge impact in the Chicagoland area and beyond.

What is even more exciting is the meeting we have in mid October with ABC. Here I am minding my own business with my producer in a downtown high rise. He says to me, that is Oprah over there, would you like to meet her? Absolutely! He introduces us and to my surprise – she is familiar with my show and loves it! You can't make this stuff up!

Elizabeth Fitzpatrick

The trip back to my 30-year class reunion is bittersweet for me. The kids, now ages 17 and 15, aren't coming back with Bill and me. They both have big athletic tournaments they can't miss this weekend. In fact, Bill and I really shouldn't be missing them either. We've paid a lot of money to get our kids in premier sports and it's so competitive out there that if they miss a practice or game they may be cut.

Good thing Bill got his pilot's license three years ago, so we don't have to drive everywhere. He and I are flying into West Plaines municipal airport Saturday morning to visit Mom and Dad, go the reunion for a few hours and then fly back to Denver that night. We don't want to miss our kids' championship tournaments the next day.

Bill's pilot license really came in handy a few months ago when Kevin Brown passed away. When Mom and Dad called to let me know he passed, initially I had no plans to attend his funeral. Since it was spring break and the kids didn't have any games, Bill flew us back.

Poor Sue Ellen, she was devastated. To make matters even worse, she never really had a career. If something were to happen to Bill – it would be really tough on our family. But financially, I would be just fine – assuming I had a job.

Bill and I need to leave town late Sunday night for business trips on opposite ends of the country. The kids are old enough they can take care of themselves and drive themselves to their private high school when we are both out of town.

I can't believe how much money it takes to keep the Fitzpatricks going each month! Bill and I are both at the height of our careers and are making more money than ever. But with buying our new twin engine plane a few years ago, plus renting the hangar space, moving to our new home in a trendy part of Denver (plus the renovations), the kid's private school, four vehicles – well I guess I can see where our money is going. The mountain home - at least we are splitting with some friends - but we never seem to go there. Or if we go, we fly into Steamboat Springs for one day like we are handling this weekend back in West Plaines.

Sometimes I've thought about cutting back my hours. Melissa's last year of high school is next year and Aaron is only two years behind her. That time has flown by. When I talk to Bill about it, all he says is "What are you willing to give up if our income drops? Plus, you won't be as valuable to the oil company as a part-time Chief Financial Officer. They may let you go all together."

That is always a fear of mine. What if I was let go from my position? While Bill and I make a lot of money (me more), we really have not saved for retirement, college, or even a rainy day. We've always been able to "earn our way" out of everything.

Maybe I'm being silly. There is no way they would ever let me go. Plus, we've always been able to earn our way out before, so why would now be any different?

I wonder how Michaels did with the advice and strategic plan I helped him put together. I hear through the grapevine he left the financial advisory business. Would love to see Laura again!

And of course, I always look forward to seeing Gary and Carol Davidson. Now they owe me big time! I feel responsible for that union plus I've been supporting them with more paintings for our new home and mountain home, plus all the people I have referred them.

Chapter 7 discussion questions:

What was your reaction to Kevin's accident?

_____

_____

What was Sue Ellen's attitude?

_____

_____

Elizabeth's biggest fear was losing her high-paying job. What do you fear losing that keeps you from what you really want?

_____

_____

Chapter 8 – The City Park

Gary Davidson

We sure picked a beautiful day for the picnic. The West Plaines City Park never looked so good. I remember back in school when the city park was kind of a joke. It was literally a place to go park, not much more than a vacant lot at the edge of town. Now it is manicured with flowers, playground equipment, park benches, and even a gazebo. I understand that they even have concerts here once a month in the summer. It is exciting to see what the townspeople have done with this little burg. I am guessing that Kevin and the other people who grew up here, and stayed, decided they could make this a nice place if they all pitched in and worked hard.

The bad part, of course is the news of Kevin's death. I can't believe he is gone. It seems like he was just starting to make his mark on the community when his life was snuffed out. It certainly makes you want to live each day to the fullest. One never knows when that proverbial farm truck will pull out in front of you.

At the 20th reunion, Kevin seemed unmotivated, but something changed. He and Sue Ellen became the pillars of the community and seemed to be involved in about everything from the city council to the school board, and now he's gone.

Of course, my life is about 180 degrees from where I was ten years ago too. For one thing I am now married. Carol is not only my wife, but my business manager, encourager, and muse. She is also my spiritual mentor.

I know that the husband is supposed to be the spiritual head of the house, but when we met, Carol was a Christian and I wasn't. In fact, I didn't even know what a Christian was. She didn't insist that I go to church with her or anything like that; it is just that she had all of these friends, and I, being new in town, didn't know a soul.

There were pot luck suppers, concerts, seminars, and all sorts of social events that we went to. The people were all so friendly and loving. I soon figured out that these were mainly people from Carol's church, so I started going with her just to see my new friends. A lot of the stuff the preacher said didn't make sense to me, but some of it did.

When some of our friends asked us to join a Bible study group, I jumped at the chance. Carol was shocked; she didn't think I would go. At the Thursday evening group we spent about thirty minutes praying, about an hour studying the Bible, and another thirty minutes just shooting the bull. A lot of the people were artists and musicians, so I really enjoyed talking with them. At first I never prayed out loud, but eventually I got brave enough to say a few words. Before long, I was leading in prayer. I couldn't believe myself.

I was baptized as an adult three years ago and I am now on the "art" committee at our church. I am now teaching painting to fourth graders this summer. That is an experience.

Sue Ellen Brown

I was kind of holding my breath to see what Kevin's classmates would think of our little town. I heard a few sour comments about missing the Town Tavern, or wondering why we tore down the old water tower, but most were very positive.

Ten years ago Kevin was sort of ashamed of the fact that he never left West Plaines. His friend, Elizabeth, was a big shot with an oil company, while I was checker at Walmart.

Elizabeth is still a big shot and I am still at Walmart, but so what? I know this still isn't much of a town by some standards, but being a big fish in a small pond isn't all that bad. In fact, Kevin and I liked having people wave at us when we drove down the street and having people stop us to discuss some city business. I doubt if even big city mayors like Richard Daly feel any better about their city than Kevin did about West Plaines.

I am particularly happy about how the city park turned out, or I should say, is turning out. It is an ongoing project of course, and has become a sort of symbol of the "new" West Plaines. I am particularly pleased it is being renamed "Brown Park." I am going to push for "Kevin Brown Park" to be more specific. There are other Browns around, but there was only one Kevin. He was certainly unique and I sure do miss him.

The big surprise at the picnic was that Gary Davidson has become a Christian. I haven't got my head around the idea that an old pot-smoking hippy can become a Christian. I go to church every week and all, but I don't see many people changed as much as Gary has in the last ten years. He still is an artist in every sense of the word, but his priorities, purpose, and even personality have changed a great deal. He and Carol suggested they go to church with me and the kids tomorrow and then take us out to eat at the new restaurant. I guess it is their turn to buy.

Ten years ago when Gary stopped by for lunch, I never would have guessed that we would be in this position. He is happily married, a Christian, and I am a widow. We certainly have a lot to talk about.

Ben Michaels

The first person I saw at the picnic was Gary Davidson. There was this dude smiling at me when we entered the park and his eyes lit up when he saw me. When I realized it was Davidson, I thought he was looking at someone behind me!

He told me he had been meaning to call me because he and his wife Carol were in Chicago a few years ago at an art show. He said he heard me on the radio.

Before this reunion, he Googled me and found out I was doing a new television show in Chicago called the "Happy Husband." I didn't even know he was married, but I met his wife Carol and they are a dynamite couple!

Of course, Laura and Carol hit it off right away and they sat down to visit while Gary and I kept talking. I went on to tell him about the show and how the radio show led to the television show. Ten years ago, I would never have dreamed I would do a show about being a happy husband! I was recovering from a nasty divorce.

I asked Gary how his marriage was going and he just beamed. I couldn't get over how different he looked – not only his outside appearance but his inner personality. I told him how I was planning to do a segment on men who married later in life. It dawned on me to interview him on my show – and he agreed!

He also thought this would be great for his art business – and I couldn't have agreed more. It really made me feel good to help him out in this way. Plus, I think he will make a great guest.

Elizabeth Fitzpatrick

We got to the picnic and the first person I wanted to talk to was Ben Michaels - for two reasons - to see what he did with my goal setting help and to see if he was still married to Laura.

The last time I talked with Ben, he and Laura had been married for about five years. I have to tell you, I was really proud of him for not messing that one up. He definitely "married up."

So, we entered the city park, which was much nicer than ten years ago by the way, and who were Ben and Laura talking to? Gary and Carol! I couldn't believe it. After we walked up to both couples, Gary and Carol greeted us first. Gary thought we were skipping the reunion, since we were back for Kevin's funeral. But I reminded him that Bill is a pilot and I have a plane now. At first, I thought he'd give me a funny look, but he said that was pretty cool. Hmmm…

He told me he was asked to be on a television show called the "Happy Husband." Any more, I'm not always sure when Gary is kidding or not. So, I cautiously asked him to tell me more about that. He told me Ben hosts the television show in Chicago! Bill started cracking up, saying he could totally see Ben doing that. I can too, but it kind of surprised me. I jokingly said to Gary that my goal setting help must have really helped Ben. Or maybe I wasn't joking. I dislike that part of myself – envy. I couldn't genuinely be happy for Ben without elevating myself.

Bill started talking to Gary, while Carol and I caught up. She seemed really happy and once again I found myself taking credit for their union. I guess I thought I would be less like this as I accomplished more in my life. I actually feel like I've gotten worse and this scares me a little.

After Carol shared with me how happy she and Gary were, it reminded me of Kevin and Sue Ellen at our 20-year reunion. While Bill and I are still married, I don't feel like we are closer. Because the kids are bigger, Bill and I tend to be around each other less. Is that why we get along better?

I decided I wasn't in the mood to talk to Ben and Laura, so Bill and I left the picnic early to visit my parents. Maybe, we can catch up with them tonight at the reunion. I also want to make sure I stop by to see Sue Ellen while we are in West Plaines.

Chapter 8 discussion questions:

Have you had a spiritual experience similar to Gary's?

_____

_____

Why and how did Gary's attitude toward Ben change? What did they have in common at their 30-year reunion that they did not have at their 20-year reunion?

_____

_____

Elizabeth thought envy in her life would reduce as she became older and more mature. What area in your life had you hoped would be better by now?

_____

_____

Chapter 9 – VFW Hall

Sue Ellen Brown

I hadn't intended to go to the banquet at the VFW, but I was given a special invitation and everybody insisted that I be there, so I went. I soon found out what the fuss was all about. The highlight of the evening was the unveiling and presentation of a huge sign that will be at the entrance to the city park. It is a large natural colored wooden sign with big letters, "KEVIN BROWN MEMORIAL PARK."

I really don't know what Kevin would have said, but he must be pleased looking down from heaven. The last few years we talked a lot about leaving a legacy. Will future generations know we were even here? Would we make a difference to those coming after us? Not necessarily having a park named after us, but would this place be a better place because of something we did?

Elizabeth got up after the presentation and commented about what a great guy Kevin was and how this was a fitting memorial. I am sure that she didn't know about the struggles getting the bond issue passed for the improvements. She probably hadn't heard about the resistance from some of the townspeople about spending their tax money on something as frivolous as a park.

She also made an odd comment about doubting if anyone would ever name a park after her. It was almost like she was admitting her life was only about her and all the stuff she has. Her name would never be associated with a place for families to gather to play ball and have picnics. Those weren't exactly the words she used, but that is what I heard, and I think other people heard the same thing based on what I heard people saying later at Walmart.

The last time Kevin and Gary were together they talked about their lives being a garden and their desire to plant things that would last. Kevin was thinking about buildings that would be around for generations and Gary was talking about art that might be in a gallery five-hundred years from now. But the real legacy will be the lives they touched, not just through things they created, but through the people who are different because they knew them.

Ben Michaels

We got my kids settled at Mom's and headed down to the alumni banquet at the VFW hall. Laura asked who we were sitting with and I had no idea. Ten years ago, we sat with Elizabeth and Bill. We didn't even talk to them at the picnic today – which was kind of weird.

Laura asked how I felt about sitting with Gary and Carol. I thought that would be great. Once we walked in, Elizabeth came up to us and said hello. She also mentioned we did not have a class representative to speak on our behalf and whether I wanted to do it again. While I know I'd do a great job – I suggested she represent our class.

She asked if I was sure and I was. Laura told me she was impressed that I turned that over to Elizabeth. I was actually pretty impressed myself. My need to be exalted has really tamed down.

After we put our things at the table, we spotted Sue Ellen at the reunion. We couldn't believe it. So we walked over to Sue Ellen and reintroduced ourselves, hugged her, and gave our condolences.

Laura said exactly the right things to Sue Ellen and I could tell Sue Ellen really appreciated it. I told her what a great job Kevin and the city council had done in West Plaines. I especially thought the city park was top notch. We both thanked her for coming.

While we were talking with Sue Ellen, Gary and Carol walked up. Sue Ellen is really fond of that couple. Not sure when/where they became so close. I missed it, but maybe Gary and Kevin connected at the last reunion. I know they were not buddies in high school.

We ended up sitting with Gary and Carol and once the program started, the emcee for the banquet asked Sue Ellen to come to the podium. This is where they presented the "KEVIN BROWN MEMORIAL PARK" sign to her in honor of Kevin.

I have to tell you, that really impacted me and brought home the void in our reunion since Kevin passed away. I was so glad I was not representing our class tonight. I don't think I could have gotten through it without bawling like a baby.

When it was our class's chance to be represented, I thought Elizabeth did a really nice job blending our class with the award given to Kevin today. Both Laura and I commented that Elizabeth seemed to have some regret about something as she spoke. Was it because she and Kevin dated in high school, or something bigger?

Gary Davidson

Carol and I had a good time with Sue Ellen talking about Kevin. Carol didn't know Kevin, but after meeting Sue Ellen, I think she has a pretty good idea of who he was.

I didn't realize the influence I had on him until Sue Ellen began to tell me about how Kevin had changed after our conversation about our mind being a garden. We talked about how we were all born with seeds planted and it was our job to cultivate the good stuff and pull out the weeds. The challenge in life is to be able to tell which is which.

Sue Ellen said that after I left they talked about that for a long time. Kevin always thought that he was some sort of a weed himself stuck in a backwater town like West Plaines. As he and Sue Ellen talked, they began to see West Plaines as a garden itself that just needed to be cultivated.

Kevin realized that he wasn't a weed, but might just be a good plant struggling to get a good start. He had roots that were deep in the area, but no blooms. Kevin stood up and shouted, "We need to bloom where we are planted." I don't remember saying that, but Sue Ellen said that is what Kevin heard me say, and it became his new motto.

That is when he started taking pride in this little town and began to work to make things better.

Kevin was a big influence on me also. When I saw how happy he and Sue Ellen were, even in modest surroundings, I began to see what was missing in my life. I guess I was thinking about what I had missed not having a wife, as I was driving to Santa Fe that Sunday after the 20th reunion.

I don't want to say that Carol was the first woman I saw after that conversation, but the irony is that I think she was. In a larger sense, she was the first woman that I really saw - the first person that I wanted to spend the rest of my life with.

When I saw Ben Michaels at the picnic, I tried to ignore him, but then a voice inside me said, "No, give him another chance, things are different." Actually, I don't know who has changed the most, him or me. He looked the same and sounded the same, but he wasn't quite the egotist that he was, or maybe I am more tolerant. I know I had a pretty big chip on my shoulder at our 20th. I was insecure with who I was and the old Gary was everything I didn't want to be.

Now, I am comfortable in my own skin and that is huge. I have mellowed too. Either that or Ben wasn't as bad as I had remembered him.

When Carol and I were in Chicago a few years ago, we heard Ben on the radio. I wouldn't call it a "monster" show, but it was legit. I told him about listening to him and even considered giving him a call. Carol wanted me to, but I still had too many bad feelings.

At this reunion, we talked about how our lives had changed. I told him about Carol, our marriage, the art business, and my new life in Christ. He invited me to be on his new television show. I told him that it would be awhile before we would be in Chicago again.

Elizabeth and her husband, Bill, flew in from Denver. They have their own plane, but Elizabeth made sure we knew it was "her" plane and Bill is the pilot. She said it as if Bill worked for her as her personal pilot, but that is probably not the way she meant it. Now I know somebody who flies their own plane. I suppose that you can make a good argument for having a private plane. If you travel a lot and spend a lot of time sitting around airports, being hassled by the TSA, the idea of just jumping on your own plane and flying to places the airlines don't go, like West Plaines, does have its appeal.

Before I met Carol, I would have said that a private plane was just stupid and never give it another thought. Carol would quickly come up with some sort of hourly operating cost schedule compared to time lost driving or waiting in airports and conclude that it may or may not be smart move to have a private plane. She would have an Excel spreadsheet to prove something that seems pretty obvious to me without much thought.

That's why we make such a good couple and perfect business partners. I see things abstractly and can make a decision with very little or no information, while she analyzes everything in detail to reach about the same conclusion. That's my perspective, not hers. She would say that I jump to conclusions without thinking things through.

I am looking forward to getting back to work. I have some new ideas and seem a little rejuvenated by getting back to my roots. Carol was a good sport and seemed to enjoy herself, even though she didn't know a soul except for me and Elizabeth, who she hadn't seen for years. She mingles easily and is everybody's new best friend. Everybody loves her, but sometimes people don't know how to take me - but I am getting better. Meeting new people isn't one of my natural abilities, but I think I am teachable.

I am learning that just because I am an artist doesn't mean that I shouldn't make friends or become a salesperson. I am learning that because someone is a good business person doesn't mean that they can't be sensitive or compassionate, or that a construction worker, like Kevin, can't be a good politician, in the positive sense, and make things happen.

We are all different and have different gifts, but we can't use that as an excuse for not stretching ourselves or doing things that are hard for us. Furthermore, I have learned that we can't rely on past experiences to predict what will happen in the future. As the financial guys say, "Past performance is not an indicator of future returns." In fact, if anything, we know that "things change."

I could no more go to the top floor office of the chairman of a major company and sell him a painting (like my wife can) than I could jump out his window and fly. But in God's strength, I can stand around in the gallery and chat with that executive about my art, while Carol moves in for the close. It takes both of us.

God is certainly in control. In our own strengths, we are stuck with what we can see and our past experiences. God has infinite wisdom and can see beyond our circumstances to the way things could be. We need to put Him in the driver's seat of our lives and enjoy the ride.

As I talked with Ben about the TV interview, it became more obvious that I would need to go to

Chicago. I like Chicago, but I can't get excited about paying $50 to park my car or $100 for dinner. That is just not something I will ever get used to.

When Ben told me that expenses were all on him, I had a little change of attitude. Carol quickly added that we needed to contact a gallery in Chicago to tie in with the program so we could use the show to promote a gallery opening. Cool!

Now I know why I spent those years struggling in Lawrence trying to sell art at fairs. I didn't have people like Carol, or even Ben, around to help me get into marketing. We certainly do need each other, and it takes all kinds of people to make these things work.

Of course, I am still nervous as I can be about being on television, telling people what a great husband I am. The truth is I am just old hippy that met Jesus and a wonderful woman. I had absolutely nothing to do with it. Left to my own devices I would still be smoking pot and driving an old Subaru instead of signing autographs and driving a new Volvo.

Elizabeth Fitzpatrick

Bill and I arrived at the VFW Hall early because we were flying back to Denver about 10:00 that night. We received a call from our 15-year-old son and his lacrosse team made it to the finals in his tournament the next morning. It's a good thing we have the plane for times like this, but I really was torn leaving so quickly. Sometimes I wonder if we do have too much going on – and what impact will all this have on our kids' lives?

Since I was the first one there, the emcee asked if we had a class representative and I said I would take care of it – thinking Ben would do it again. He didn't, so it was up to me.

Sue Ellen was there, too. I was so glad because I would not have been able to see her otherwise. She thanked both Bill and me for attending the funeral a few months ago. I'm so glad we made the trip back.

When I asked Sue Ellen why she was at the reunion, she told me about the award for Kevin. I was shocked and thrilled at the same time. I mentioned I was the class representative tonight and knowing about the award made it all the more special.

As we walked over to our table, Bill commented how genuinely concerned I was for Sue Ellen. I thanked him and then thought to myself – why was that different? Is it because of Sue Ellen's loss or because she is not a threat to me? I really need to get to the bottom of this, because I don't like the way I am sometimes around other successful people.

After I spoke for our class, several people came up to me and thanked me. They also said I did a nice job – which I already knew. Yet, I had a really empty feeling inside of me. I even said, in front of everyone, that I was concerned whether I had done anything of lasting value like Kevin did. What would people say about me if I were to die today?

Chapter 9 discussion questions:

Who are the significant people in your life who complement your abilities and vice versa?

_____

_____

What are you doing now that will have an impact on others 100 years from now or for eternity?

_____

_____

If you were to die today, what would people say at your funeral? Is this what you want for your life?

_____

_____